MIA CLARK

ISBN: 1511599049
ISBN-13: 978-1511599047

*Book design by Cerys du Lys*
*Cover design by Cerys du Lys*
*Cover Image © Depositphotos | avgustino*

Cherrylily.com

# DEDICATION

Thank you to Ethan and Cerys for helping me with this book and everything involved in the process. This is a dream come true and I wouldn't have been able to do it without them. Thank you, thank you!

# CONTENTS

# ACKNOWLEDGMENTS

Thank you for taking a chance on my book!

I know that the stepbrother theme can be a difficult one to deal with for a lot of people for a variety of reasons, and so I took that into consideration when I was writing this. While this is a story about forbidden love, it's also a story about two people becoming friends, too. Sometimes you need someone to push you in your life, even when you think everything is fine. Sometimes you need someone to be there, even when you don't know how to ask them to stay with you.

This is that kind of story. It is about two people becoming friends, and then becoming lovers. The forbidden aspects add tension, but it's more than that, too. Sometimes opposites attract in the best way possible. I hope you enjoy my books!

# STEPBROTHER WITH BENEFITS

## 1 - Ethan

YEAH, WELL, what do you want me to do? I was hungry, she was hungry, so we went to get some food. French fries to be specific.

I drive us there, while Ashley just sits in the passenger seat, kind of calm, relaxed. She seems real chill right now, which I can get behind. It's nice. I've always thought of her as kind of uptight and snooty, but not in a bad way. It's just the way she is, just like I'm the way I am. That's not going to change. There's no reason for it to change.

Right now she's just more... fuck if I know. She's got the window rolled down, the wind sweeping through her hair like we're driving along some country road, going camping for the weekend to get away from it all, just for a little bit. It's nice. It's how I like to feel all the time, but lately it's getting harder and harder. I can't explain that one; or, seriously, I don't want to explain it to you. This is my time, not yours.

I pull up to the place and park our ride. I borrowed one of my dad's nicer cars, but nothing too fancy. We're here for french fries and to hang out, not get gaped at by a bunch of annoying kids who want to ask all sorts of stupid questions about the car. I like cars, alright? Yeah, they're cool, and sometimes they're cool as fuck, but I'm busy right now.

I turn off the car and Ashley's just sitting there, not a care in the world. Yeah, that's probably my fault. It happens sometimes. After I give a girl explosive orgasms and amazing sex they sort of go into a daze. What can you do? I'm kind of proud of it, myself. Means I did it right.

I get out, close the door, and walk around to her side. I open her door for her and hold out my hand. Finally she snaps out of it, but just barely. She stares at me, wide-eyed and confused, then reaches for my hand. I help her up and out of the car, then close the door behind her.

"Did you just open the door for me?" she asks.

"Yeah?" I say. What the fuck is that look on her face for?

"I didn't know you did that kind of thing."

"What kind of thing are you referring to?" I ask.

"Um... the nice thing? Gentlemanly thing? I don't know."

"Listen, Princess, I know you have some preconceptions about me, and yeah, I know I'm kind of a dick, or an asshole, or whatever, but I'm not all bad. Sometimes a guy has to open a door for a lady, and this was one of those times."

She... well, what the fuck? She smiles and starts giggling. "*Ethan Colton,*" she says, all sassy and sharp. "Did you just call me a lady?"

"*Ashley Banks,*" I say, miming her sass with some of my own. "Apparently you don't realize you're classy as fuck."

"Nice," she says, rolling her eyes. "Real nice, Ethan."

"Yeah, I have a way with words," I say.

She smiles, then gives me a curtsey. Fuck, I love it. It's cute and classy, and it makes me hard. Yeah, maybe that's strange. I don't know. Every fucking thing she does seems to make me hard lately. It's like some pent up erection that's been building for...

I don't know. Awhile. Go away. I'm busy.

"Thank you," she says. "No one's ever opened a door for me like that before."

"Yeah, well, I figured you needed it," I say. "You've been kind of out of it after out little pool table session. Orgasms do that sometimes."

She blushes. Fuck, that's hot. Then she hits my shoulder, and looks all around. No one's here. It's just us in the parking lot. Even if someone saw us, so what? It's not like we're talking loud. No one can hear.

And if they heard us? I don't know. Maybe it wouldn't be so bad. Maybe it would. I'll figure it out later.

"Shhh," she says. "Ethan, I can't believe you said that."

I shrug, nonchalant. "Just teasing you, Princess. What's a brother for, right?"

She gives me another funny look, but this one is more confusing. What's she thinking? I think she's thinking about what I'm thinking and...

Yeah, she really doesn't want to know. What I'm thinking is what it'd be like to spin her around, rip down her pants, and fuck her right here and now over the hood of the car. Obviously I'm not going to do that. I'm not that barbaric. I'll wait until we're back home and parked in the garage. Not exactly the same, but it'll have to do.

"You want to go inside or just stand here chatting all day?" I ask.

The look fades. A little. She still looks at me weird, but she gives in and smiles, too. "Alright," she says.

We walk inside, seat ourselves at a booth, and wait for someone to come serve us.

I even opened the restaurant door for her, too. Thought I could get a blush out of her or something. Fuel this raging hard-on trapped in my pants, give me something to look forward to later. But, nah, she does something even worse.

No blushing, but she shakes her ass a little, giving me a show. Fuck, I can't do this. I can't fucking do this. I bite my lip to stop myself from doing anything out of line, but it's hard. It's real hard. Just a little... *smack*. How satisfying would that be?

I don't know if Ashley knows this, but there's two things I find irrevocably sexy in a woman. I already told her the first one: it's class. Ashley is not trashy by any means, and she never has been. No, she doesn't come from a rich family like mine, even though she's kind of stuck in one now, but she's always had this air of sophistication about her that I've...

Fuck you, I'm done with that shit.

The second one rhymes with class, and she just showed me that one, too. Not that I haven't noticed it before, but I've had to restrain myself, you know? Fuck, this is my sister now.

Stepsister. Is there a difference? Yeah, kind of, but barely.

Anyways, class and ass. Two very admirable and arousing attributes. They both make me hard. So fucking hard.

Why'd we go out to eat again? I wish we'd ordered in. I only have a week with her and I feel like I'm missing out. If my cock isn't buried deep inside her pussy, it's just a fucking waste.

# 2 - *Ashley*

HEY HUN," the waitress says to me, then to Ethan, she adds, "Sweetie. What can I get for you two?"

"French fries," Ethan says.

"With gravy and curd cheese," I add.

He gives me a curious look, then adds, "And sauteed mushrooms and green peppers on top."

The waitress grins at our in sync ordering. "Anything to drink?"

Ethan defers to me first. "Can I get um..." I hesitate, because I'm not sure how this is going to go, but I've wanted to do it ever since high school, and I feel like this is my only chance. "Can I get a root beer float?" I ask.

"Sure thing," the waitress says, writing it down on her little notepad. "How about you? Maybe two straws for the float?"

Ethan blinks, clearly caught off guard. "Yeah, maybe?" he says. "Sure. Can I get a water with that, too."

"Two straws and water," the waitress says, writing all of that down. "Anything else?"

I shake my head, no. I think that's it, right? Ethan surprises me by saying, "A large steak and cheese bomb, too. Add pickles, mayo, and hot peppers to that."

I lift one brow at him, but wait until the waitress leaves to put in our order before saying anything.

"I thought we were just getting french fries?" I ask. "Are you hungry?"

"You have no fucking idea," he says, staring at me. The way he says it and the way he stares, well...

He's not talking about food, is he? I catch him staring at my breasts, even though I'm just wearing a plain white t-shirt and a pair of faded jeans. Nothing special, nothing all that attractive, but the way Ethan's looking at me I feel like...

Like his Princess. Like I'm the only thing he sees. Like we're the only two people in this building, maybe the only two people in the city, or the world, or the entire universe.

I blush and look away, but when I look back he's still staring at me the same as he was before.

"Ethan..." I say, whispered. I'm not sure what else to say, though. It's not like I can um... explain?

There's people sitting all around us, and I know they'd hear me.

"Yeah?" he says, oblivious. I don't know if it's intentional or not, but if I had to guess I'd say it is.

I take a risk. I don't know why. Maybe someone can see us. We have a large booth big enough for four, maybe six people for a tight squeeze. I scoot as far in as I can, and use my eyes to kind of direct him to do the same. He grins and moves over, like this is our shared secret. Which, it is, but I've got more to share with him, too.

I kick one of my shoes off, leaving my foot bare except for my thin socks, then I tap at his foot. Casual and smooth, he glances down quick, but then looks back up at me, nothing doing. I go further, stretching my leg out and up, teasing up along his jeans, towards his knee, and then I fake a yawn to make it easier to stretch and lean back a little.

My daring, risky foot slides onto the seat bench, then between Ethan's legs, further still until...

Oh my God he has an erection. Ethan Colton, my darling stepbrother, who really should not have an erection right now, um... well, he does. And my foot is touching it. Massaging it even. He rests one elbow on the table, keeping his hand up and propping his chin on it, but the other goes under, to his lap. He grabs my foot by the ankle, holding me in place.

Well, um... that didn't exactly go according to plan. Not that I had a plan to begin with, but now I'm stuck here, my foot in his crotch, his cock hard and ready, with my toes teasing and toying with his erection.

And, um... I kind of like it?

I grow bold, because what else can I do.

"I'm glad we're back home," he says, acting like we aren't doing something insane right now.

"Are you really?" I ask. "Because we've never really hung out before now."

"Nah, that's not true," he says.

"Ethan, it's kind of true. You only used to spend time with me when we were doing family things with all of us together, me and Mom and you and your Dad."

"And it was nice," he says.

"It *was* nice," I agree. "I just always got the feeling that you'd rather be doing something else instead. You never really seemed like you wanted to be there."

"It's complicated," he says.

I'm still massaging his cock with my foot, but I belatedly realize he's not holding my ankle anymore. I could pull back, I could go back to normal, but...

Well, what fun would that be? Yes, I'm a good girl, but I want to be a little bad for once. Just for now, just for this week. It's not going to hurt anything, right?

Any*thing*, I think. Yes, maybe not. Any*one*, though?

I've seen it happen before. A lot. Once my mom married Ethan's dad, I got more of an up close and personal view of it, too. Ethan hurt a lot of girls. I don't know if he meant to, but does that make it any better? Everyone knows how he is. *Everyone*. He sleeps with girls, and by all accounts they think he's amazing.

For a week or two.

And then he stops calling them, doesn't answer their calls, either. No more texts. If he sees them in public, he just sort of brushes them off. Says that it's over, he's got other things to do. I remember one girl from our class coming to his dad's mansion late at night, crying and banging on the door. I was supposed to be asleep, but I snuck out and listened from the top of the stairs.

Ethan's dad told my mom that this wasn't the first time this has happened. My mom offered to talk to the girl for a little while before bringing her home. I'm not sure if Ethan's dad liked that idea or not, but my mom did it anyways. They went into the den to sit down, and then I couldn't hear them anymore so I started to tiptoe back to my room, and...

I saw him. Ethan. He was at his door, just standing there, watching me. As soon as I saw him, he just... he looked at me. Not happy, not sad, just stared at me. Then he stepped back into his room without a word and closed the door behind him. A second later I heard the lock click shut, trapping him inside.

I think I hated him. I think I've always hated him, but I don't know for sure.

That night, I wasn't sure if I did or not. He looked so indifferent and... maybe not hateful in an active and aggressive way, but more in an indifferent and passive way. Uncaring, I guess is a better way to explain it, but hate is hate, regardless.

I just never could figure out who Ethan hated. A part of me has always wondered if maybe he hates himself for what he does?

Obviously that's stupid. I have no right to judge him. I'm attending college for English with a specialization in historical texts, not Psychology.

I've just always felt like there's more to Ethan Colton, but I don't know what.

Right now there's a lot more, and currently it's twitching and throbbing as I rub my foot against it.

"You alright?" Ethan asks. "You look kind of out of it."

"Oh, um... I'm just thinking," I say.

I don't know if I want to explain to him or not, so I redouble my efforts on his crotch. I tease up his shaft with my toes and the side of my foot, then around to the other side. It's a little hard, what with his pants keeping him confined, but that makes it fun, too. *A little hard?* No, um... Ethan is very hard right now.

For me. He told me this before, but I found it difficult to believe. Now, though? Um... I'm definitely becoming a believer.

"Why did you make me pancakes?" I ask.

He gives me a weird look, but I see something more in his eyes. Something telling, but I don't know what exactly it means.

"I was hungry," he says. "I was just making breakfast."

"No you weren't," I say. "You could have just made eggs and sausage, but you made pancakes, too."

He glares at me, almost angry, but not quite. "I just wanted to make some fucking pancakes," he says.

"You didn't make them because they're my favorite?" I ask.

"What the fuck do I care what your favorite breakfast is?" he says.

I press my foot hard into his crotch, teasing him even more, though um... maybe a bit rougher than I should.

Ethan's nostrils flare and he glares at me harder. "Stop asking questions like that," he says.

"No," I say, petulant. "I won't. Also, why did you offer to have a night in with me last night? Why did you..."

I'm not sure what I want to say. The drinking? Well, we're both underage, and we're in public, so... but also the sex? The dare? Why did he agree to my dare? I wouldn't have held him to it. I don't want him to quit football or anything. We were both tipsy, so...

"You looked like you needed to get shitface drunk," he says. "And I needed someone to drink with. Would be fucked up if I did it alone, don't you think?"

"Ethan!" I hiss at him.

"No one fucking cares about two rich kids drinking at home, Princess. Get a fucking life."

Why's he being so rude all of a sudden? I don't know, but I intend to put a stop to it right here and now!

If he's going to make our underage drinking public, I'm going to... well, not exactly, but...

"Rule number twelve," I say, caressing his cock with my foot while I speak. "You can't be mean to me. Not for this entire week."

He smirks. "I know you think that's cute and funny," he says. "You're forgetting who I am, though. You think I care about your rules?"

I want to kick him. In the balls. And I could. Right here and now. I'd have some explaining to do to someone, and I might not have a ride home after since I'm pretty sure Ethan would get up, get in the car, and leave me here, but...

"You will," I say to him. I'm not sure if I'm calling his bluff or just stating a fact. "Ethan, I just want to know. Rule number seven, right?"

He furrows his brow, so I add, "It's the no lying one."

"I think that rule was specifically for you, Princess," he says, but the tone of his voice is uncertain and unsure, like maybe he doesn't believe what he's saying.

I think the rule was supposed to be for me, too, but I want it to be for him, as well.

"Rule number thirteen," I say, as confidently as I can. "All of the rules should apply to both of us evenly."

He grins, cocksure and confident. This is the Ethan I know. Well, the Ethan I know is also a prick, so him being a jerk before was kind of also the Ethan I know. It's just... I feel like the Ethan from the past couple of days is different. I feel like I know two of him now, two entirely different ones, and...

I don't know which is the real one. I'm not sure if there is a real one. Maybe I'm giving him too much credit and I'm wrong about a lot of what's going on.

"How's that going to work with rule number eleven?" he asks.

Eleven? Oh, um...

I blush, but I tease at his cock with my foot even more, goading him on. "You'll just have to wait and see, won't you?" I ask, as seductive as I can. I hope it came out right. I hope he thinks it's sexy. I...

Our waitress comes back with our food. She places the large root beer float glass between us, two straws dangling out the top, one pointing at me and the other at Ethan. Then she places our fries down, too. Two empty plates to go along with them. Ethan gets another plate for his steak and cheese bomb, which... oh God, it smells and looks amazing. To top it all off, the waitress reaches into her apron and gives us both a set of utensils wrapped up in paper napkins.

"Just let me know if you need anything else, alright?" she says, smiling.

Ethan nods. "Yeah, sure thing."

I grab one of the empty plates for the fries and unwrap my fork and knife, but I... no, I can't. I can't say that. Can I? Um... well, I can, so...

I just blurt it out. "Can I have a bite of your sub?" I ask.

He gives me a funny look. The sub is already cut in half, so he just takes half of it, reaches across the table, and puts it in my empty plate. I stare at him, dumbfounded, not sure what's going on.

"Yeah," he says, as if he didn't already answer me with his actions. "You can."

"An entire half?" I ask.

"What's with the questions?" he asks.

"I don't know. It's just weird. You're being weird."

He bites into his sandwich, chews, and swallows, then he looks at me. It's sort of a cross between a stare and a glare, but then a gaze, and... I don't know. It's very intense and hard to look away from.

"Listen, alright, because I'm only going to say this once, and I don't want you getting any ideas from it," he says. "You listening?"

I nod, quiet.

"I made you those fucking pancakes because I know you like pancakes. Yeah, do you have a problem with that? I did it on purpose. I asked you if you wanted to stay in and get drunk last night, because I thought it'd help you feel better and I knew you'd never come up with the idea on your own, because you're too much of a fucking Goodie Two-Shoes Little Miss Perfect Princess. You need to just fucking relax and calm the fuck down sometimes. I've seen you stress out over the stupidest shit, Ashley."

I open my mouth to say something, to protest, but he stops me.

"Also, I ordered this on purpose, too. You know when we order out sometimes? And we're all looking at the menu? You, me, your mom, my dad? Yeah, you think no one noticed. You always order a fucking salad, but I see you drooling over the steak and cheese subs, so yeah, I ordered this because I knew you'd want half, and you'd never get it on your own. I got the pickles, the mayo, and the hot peppers because I like them, though. So there you go. Rule number fucking seven."

I blush and look away from him and... did he really? For all of that? I don't understand, though. I don't know how he knows some of these things, or... no, it makes sense. The first two make sense, at least. Not the steak and cheese bomb. That one confuses me. Has he been...?

No. Unlikely. I must have been really obvious, and now that I think back on it, I probably sounded more than a little depressed when saying that I'd just have a salad. Ethan's dad would always ask me if I was sure, too, so that makes sense. It fits with what I know.

I wasn't sure, though. Not then, and not now. I wouldn't say I'm ugly or anything, but I've always been conscious of my weight, because I feel like I don't have a lot to offer, you know? Besides being intelligent, which, um... I don't think that's a high priority for most guys, but... I just wanted to try and look nice. Look better. Not that it worked. I was too scared to wear clothes that fit me better, to show off my figure a little so boys in school might be attracted to me more.

No one even asked me out until I went to college, and to be completely honest I'm not even sure why they did then. I don't stand out, except for my grades. Maybe that was it. Maybe they just wanted to use me as a study buddy, with making out and maybe sex on the side. It wouldn't surprise me, because I feel like that's basically exactly what happened.

Until now. Sort of. I don't know. What are we doing? What's going on between us? Ethan and I...

"What's with the root beer float?" he asks, nodding at it. "Two straws, what the fuck?"

"Oh, um..." Rule number seven, right? No lying to each other. "Do you remember in high school when some boys would ask girls on dates and they'd come here but it was public so no one could make out and um... they'd get root beer floats with two straws, since if they were both drinking at the same time it was kind of like kissing?"

Ethan snatched up one of the gravy and cheese covered french fries when I started explaining, and he was chewing and swallowing halfway through, but as soon as I finish with the kissing part, he starts choking on the fry.

Oh my God, he's dying. Oh my God, I've killed him, haven't I? Why did I say that? Well, why did I do it? Because I knew what I was doing when I ordered the float, so...

But, no, Ethan grabs his glass of water and chugs fast, swallowing down the fry with the water. He stops choking, and now he's just glaring at me. Hard.

I just now realize that my foot is still pressed against his cock, and he's harder than ever.

"I think you've got the wrong fucking idea about what we're doing here, Princess," he says.

"Oh?" I ask, feigning innocence. "I don't know what you're talking about, Ethan."

"I'm just saying," he says. "When we get home, I'm going to set you straight."

Is he? Hm... I wonder what that means?

# 3 - Ethan

WE FINISH WITH OUR FOOD. It's good. I even give in to her stupid fucking girly idea about the root beer float. Kissing? What the fuck bullshit is that? It's kind of cute, though. It's definitely an Ashley thing. No idea how else to explain that one. She's so fucking sensitive and responsive, it's ridiculous, but then she does and says shit like that and it's like she wasn't just cumming around my cock, she wasn't just thrashing on the pool table while I was balls deep inside her, she wasn't just trembling from excitement when I ate her out for the very first time ever.

This girl is fucking everything any guy could ever want and I don't know why none of them can see it. None of them have ever been able to see it. It's just so fucking strange and insane to me. It's goddamn weird.

We leave the restaurant and, for fun, I open the door for her again. She sashays that beautiful fucking derriere at me, too. Is she doing that shit on purpose? I follow behind her while she heads to our car. Scoping the parking lot out, making sure no one's watching, I sneak up close and then smack her ripe little ass. She squeaks--some fucking delicious, beautiful sound--then spins around and slaps me hard.

Holy fuck, Princess has spunk. I love it. I touch my cheek where she smacked me; it stings red hot.

She stares at me, lips parted, then she gasps. "Oh my God, Ethan, I'm so sorry, I... you startled me, that's all. I didn't mean to, I swear. Are you alright?"

"Kiss it," I tell her, offering her my cheek. "Go on, kiss it better, Princess. Show me how sorry you are."

She fidgets and squirms. It's asking a lot. I wouldn't blame her if she doesn't do it. I don't actually think she'll do it, but just for fun I add something else.

"I dare you," I say.

There it is. Determination in her eyes. And something else, too. Fuck, she's gorgeous. It's her eyes. They're as emotional as her body is responsive. They say so much, if only you take the time to listen.

She peeks around the parking lot quick, then she slips in close and kisses my cheek. I think that's it, and she pulls away after, but then she grabs my cheeks in her palms and stands up on tiptoes and she kisses me.

I grab her. It's instinctive, but only for a second, and then I realize what I'm doing, but I don't give a fuck. I hold her hips and pull her close and I kiss her back. My tongue finds hers and we dance, holding each other, kissing with passion and lust.

Yeah, I've had a hard-on this entire time. Full throbbing erection. I can't help it. This girl does shit to me that you wouldn't even understand.

Someone whistles at us, a cat call. Ashley stops kissing me and blushes, flustered, then tries to pull away, but I keep my hands on her hips, holding her close. I slip in once more, giving her a final, soft kiss, then I let her go. We both turn to look at who we just gave a show to, and it's just some random fuck. I don't know who. No one important. I don't recognize him, and he sure as fuck doesn't recognize us.

Which is good, because if he did, he'd realize I was just making out with my stepsister. And, yeah, probably not the best thing for someone to know about. I'd really rather they didn't.

It's supposed to be a guilt-free temporary thing, anyways.

We head back to the car again. She gets in her side on her own this time, and I get into the driver's seat. Doors close, we're sitting there. I put the key in the ignition, turn on the car, but just let it idle for a bit. I want to go back home, I want to lift her up over my shoulder, drag her upstairs, and fuck the shit out of her. Maybe we won't even get upstairs. I don't know.

It's just too much, though. You ever want to fuck someone so bad that when the time finally comes, it seems too good to be true? And you just don't want to ruin it, so maybe you'll wait a little longer? What's the rush, right?

This is kind of like that. Kind of. I just want to savor the fuck out of it, that's all. I don't expect you to understand, but just try, alright?

"Hey, um..." Ashley says. She's got her phone, must have pulled it out of her pocket when she got in. "Do you want to...?"

"What?" I ask. "Tell me, Princess."

She blushes and mumbles and taps on her phone, swiping through menus. "Hold on, um... don't start driving yet, alright?"

"Yeah," I say, grinning. "I'll wait."

She's so fucking adorable it hurts. Sexy as fuck, cute as a button, I want to fuck her hard and then squeeze her tight and hug her for days. Yeah, it doesn't even make sense to me. I don't know what I'm talking about anymore.

"The drive-in just started playing again this year," she says. "They opened last week. It's a double feature like always, and um..."

"Starts at sunset," I say. Everyone knows this. It's an old school kind of place. Not many left, but it's nice. Updated to try and make it more appealing, but I like the classic charm of it, too.

This is going to sound fucked up, but my favorite time to go to the drive-in was when it was slightly rainy out. Not a full on rain, because then they canceled the show for the night, but if it was just a little drizzle they risked it, and, fuck, that was the best. Real great ambiance, with the sound playing through your car radio, and the gentle pitter-patter of rain on the roof of your car, and maybe you'd turn the wipers on now and again to wipe away the rain, while the movie played on the big screen up above.

It's just nice, that's all.

"If you want to go, we um... we can?" Ashley asks.

"Listen, Princess, it sounds like you're trying to drag me out on dates or some shit," I say. Because, yeah, that's what it sounds like.

"I'm not," she says. That's it. That's all. No explanation

"Good, because that's not how this works," I say.

"How does it work, Ethan?" she asks.

What the fuck? Shouldn't it be obvious? Except, maybe not. I realize we haven't really talked about it, so maybe we should.

"I'm your stepbrother with benefits for the week," I tell her. "We're not dating or anything."

"I know," she says. "But does that mean we can't go on dates?"

"Yeah, I'm pretty sure that's what it means."

"Why?" she asks.

"What the fuck? What do you mean why?"

"I don't know," she says, but there's more to it. She knows. I know she knows.

"Just tell me," I say.

"You said this was supposed to be fun," she says. "Rule number six," she adds, mumbling.

"I meant with sex," I say. "Like if you want to try out different positions or whatever. Anal sex? I don't fucking know."

"Anal sex?" she asks, eyes wide. "Oh, um..."

"You want to?" I ask.

"I... I don't know?" she says. "I've never thought about it before."

"It's up to you. It's not for everyone. No big deal if you'd rather not."

"Maybe?" she says.

I laugh. "Yeah, sure. Maybe."

"Alright," she says, and the way she says it, the way she smiles when she says it. Fuck, she's so perfect. This is fucking me up bad.

"I don't want it to just be sex fun, though," she says. "I want to have actual fun, too."

"At the drive-in movie theatre?" I ask. "Princess, that sounds a lot like a date, except it sounds like I won't even be able to make out with you or feel you up because we'll be in public. Shitty fucking date, don't you think?"

"We can hold hands?" she offers. " We can sit in the back seat and cuddle and hold hands."

"Do you realize what you're saying right now?"

"Um, yes?"

"You're fucking cracked."

"Well, maybe, but I'd still like to go to the drive-in. It's nice, and they're playing good movies."

"It's two romantic comedy flicks, isn't it? Hit me with the news, Princess. I can take it. It's definitely two romantic comedies."

She hesitates. "No..."

"No? I don't believe you." I go to grab her phone to check for myself, but she slaps my hand away.

"It's one! It's one romantic comedy! The other one is just a regular romance. I don't think it's a funny one. It doesn't sound funny, at least."

Holy fuck. Are you kidding me? Is she for real? "So you want me to go watch a romantic comedy and some romance movie that isn't even funny? With you? When we could go home and fuck for hours instead? Because, really, I'm ready, Princess. You just say the word and I'll be in that pussy a second later."

"I would like to go to the drive-in," she says. "Please."

"I'd like to fuck you until you can't walk," I say. I don't say please, though. Who the fuck do you think I am?

Also, guess who wins? Just guess? Where do we go? Home or to the drive-in? I think the answer is pretty obvious. It should be.

# 4 - Ashley

YAY! We're at the drive-in!

I haven't been here in forever. I remember the first time I came here with my mom when I was younger. They were playing some animated movies. I forget which, but I liked them a lot. I wasn't that young, but I think about ten years old or so? We got popcorn and before the movie started I was just walking around. They have a kid's playground for younger children if they get bored sitting and watching the movie, which is neat. I walked past that, past some of the slides, past a booth with a man selling cotton candy.

On my way back to the car, I saw um... there were people kissing. Ew! *Really* kissing, too. In their cars, with the windows steaming up, and... ick.

I remember going back to the car and telling my mom and asking her why they were doing that and she just laughed at me and said I'd understand some day.

I did understand. Some day. I always kind of hoped someone in high school would ask me to the drive-in. For a date. Because...

They always played double features. Always. That was at least three hours, and sometimes four hours of movie play time. And um... *other play time...*

I did go to the drive-in sometimes, but it was with friends. We ate popcorn and actually watched the movies, and sometimes out of the corner of my eye I saw people kissing, but I tried not to notice, tried not to be jealous.

I tried. I don't think I succeeded, at least as far as wanting it to be me sometime.

Ethan laughs at my excited clap after we pay for our car to park and pull into a spot. It's mostly empty right now, but there's still a little time before the sun sets, so I'm sure it'll fill up more.

"They have cotton candy," I say.

"You want some cotton candy?" he asks.

"I didn't say that," I say in protest. "I'm just saying they have cotton candy."

"Let's go get some," he says.

"Alright!" I say, perhaps a little too excited. I did want cotton candy, but I didn't want to tell him that.

Ethan laughs at me again, then opens the door and jumps out of the car. I get out on my own this time, not waiting for him to come around and help me out. He doesn't actually move to do that, but I bet if I just sat in the car and waited, he would.

Ethan is strange. He's nice and an asshole at the same time. A nice asshole? Makes no sense. It's confusing.

We walk down the dirt path to the food stalls, side by side. I have a weird sudden urge to reach out and grab his hand, and...

Wait, maybe...

I do. I grab his hand and hold it in mine, but I swing it back and forth in a wide, sweeping arc, so it's not like we're holding hands, not for real, it's just us being silly and weird. I think something like this is fine for um... for us to do. Stepbrother and stepsister?

Ethan doesn't say anything about it, at least. He lets me do it. He squeezes my hand tight in his, too. No one else can see that, but I can feel it. I swing our arms like that once, twice, three times, back and forth, then I let go, slipping away from him.

That's it. That was fun. That's all it was. If anyone saw us, they wouldn't think too much of it. We're just fooling around. We're just...

Well, we're at the drive-in heading to get some cotton candy, that's what we're doing.

We reach the stall and Ethan gets two, one for me and one for him. His is blue and mine is pink, except they both taste the same. I pull off a puff of mine and offer it to him. He opens his mouth to accept, and I slip it onto his tongue. It's pink and looks nothing like how I imagine Ethan looking, but then he closes his mouth and swirls his tongue around, melting the sugary cotton, and the moment is lost. Gone.

I'll remember it, though. Ethan Colton with pink cotton candy. I laugh.

"You're real fucking cuddly and clingy, huh?" he asks.

"What's that supposed to mean?" I say. "Are you mad at me?"

"No," he says. "Just pointing out the obvious."

"I'm not always like this," I say. "I don't think I am."

"Nah, probably not," he says.

And, no, I'm not, I realize. I've never been like this with anyone else before. Sort of. I guess I have with my mom, though that wasn't the same, and only when I was younger. I just...

I don't know, I feel comfortable? I feel safe around Ethan, though if you asked me why, I couldn't explain it.

"It's nice," he says. "Never change, Princess."

We walk back to the car quietly after that. I start to open the front passenger door, but Ethan jerks his head to the back. "Backseat?" he asks.

"Sure," I say, smiling.

We get into the back with our cotton candy and sit. I'm far to the right at first, but Ethan is kind of halfway between the far left and the middle. I take a test scoot closer to him, then another one, and one more, until we're sitting close, side by side, my leg touching his.

"You sure you want to do that?" he asks, smirking at me.

"I don't know, do I?" I counter.

He holds his cotton candy in his left hand, but reaches to grab my thigh with his right. His fingers wrap around my leg, tight and demanding, squeezing. It's not exactly overtly sexual, but the overtones are definitely there. This is a safe sort of sexual, I guess. It's what we're allowed to do in a public setting, since no one can see us, not unless they stare right into the window.

"Ethan?" I say, looking over at him.

"What's up, Princess?" he says.

"Thank you."

"For what?"

I don't tell him. There's nothing to tell him. I just want him to know. Thank you.

# 5 - Ethan

LOOK. LISTEN UP. I don't do this. This is not what I do. This was never my plan, this isn't in the cards, if you read my zodiac for today it definitely wouldn't say anything remotely even close to whatever the fuck is happening right now.

I don't date girls; I have fun with them. I don't get cuddly, or at least I don't get any more cuddly than necessary. Yeah, alright, after you fuck a girl hard, sometimes you have to cuddle for a little while to calm them down and bring them back to the reality of what's around them. My cock has that affect on women. Not sure what else to tell you there.

I've dealt with girls like this before, too. The ones who think they can change me. They're the ones that I end it with the fastest. They're the ones that maybe get a lay or two, a couple of fun times in bed with me, and then I'm done with them. A week, max, and nothing more than that.

Well, what the fuck, that's what I'm giving Ashley, isn't it?

The problem is that it's *me* who decides this shit. I say when it's over. I say when we're done. I say what we're doing. I tell them how it's going to be, and I told her how it's going to be, too, but then what the fuck am I doing?

We're sitting in the backseat of one of my dad's cars, just hanging out, watching a movie, except it's way more than that, too. She's close. Real close. So close that if she moved away right now, the right side of my body would feel cold without her. And that's some real fucked up shit, let me tell you. I don't like it. I don't want to like it. This isn't what I do.

But I'm doing it, so what's that say about me? I have no fucking clue.

I put my arm around her shoulder and pull her even closer, and she tilts her head to the side, resting it against me. Slowly, just a little, inch by agonizing fucking inch, she reaches over and grabs my left hand, then pulls it into hers. We're holding hands, fucking cuddling, watching this stupid romantic comedy flick.

It's not so bad. The movie's alright. Can't say I hate it. It's pretty good, but it's not something I'd watch on my own. It's the type of movie I'd bring a girl to at the beginning of my week or two with them just to get them in the mood and ready for more. Light and fun, that's how I roll. Save the deep philosophical questions for someone else. Ask them to the guy who isn't going to be ignoring your calls in a couple of weeks.

"Ethan?" she says, looking up at me. "You don't like the movie, huh?"

"Nah," I say. "It's alright."

"We can just talk if you want to. We don't have to watch it. I just like it here. It's simple, you know? It doesn't feel weird or complicated. I thought it'd be nice to come here with you."

What the fuck? Yeah, I need to have a talk with her alright. Just give me a second to compose my thoughts. This is complicated.

"Look, Princess," I say. "You know me, don't you?"

She looks up at me with a strange look in her eyes. I don't like that look. "Um... yeah?"

"You know what I do. You know what we're doing. Why are you doing this to yourself?"

"Huh?"

"I don't date girls," I tell her, because it's the truth. "And we can't date, either. What's with the cuddling and shit? What's with having me bring you to see some movies at the drive-in?"

She shrugs and stiffens a little in my arm. "I know all that," she says.

"Good," I say. "Glad we got that out of the way. I just don't want you getting any expectations out of what's going on here. We've got rules to follow."

"Why do you do it?" she asks.

"Huh?"

"I don't understand why you do it," she says again. "I know maybe it's hard to find a girl you like, but you've never had a real girlfriend, have you?"

Fucking... fuck. This is new. Usually I have girls trying to talk about themselves. More specifically I usually have them trying to subtly (or not) explain to me why they're different and why they can be my first girlfriend. Instead, I've got Little Miss Perfect over here asking me why I don't find a girlfriend. Not even her, just some girl, right? What the fuck is this shit?

"You wouldn't understand," I tell her.

"I'm smart," she says. "I bet I would."

"Yeah, you're smart," I say. I can at least admit that. "It's not always about book smarts, Princess. There's a lot more to life than that."

"I know," she says.

Oh yeah? Well, good. Glad she knows. I think we're done here, then. Let's just go back to the movie.

Or not.

"I think you'd make a good boyfriend," she says. "To some girl. Not me."

"Not you?" I ask. Why did I ask that? I don't know, probably because I'm an idiot. Ashley's the smart one, remember?

"Obviously," she says. "You're my brother now."

"Yeah," I say. "Kind of fucked up how that worked out."

"What do you mean?" she asks.

Shit. "Nothing. Don't worry about it."

We go back to silently watching the movie, or so I think, but it doesn't last for long.

"What do you want to do?" she asks.

"I want to watch this movie and then go back home and fuck you," I say. Is that blatant enough? I hope so.

She laughs. Holy fuck, she laughs. I didn't think it was funny, but whatever. I guess it's a little funny.

"I meant after college. Do you have any plans? Are you going to play football professionally?"

Yeah, now it's my turn to laugh, which I do. She cuddles close to me and squeezes my hand, though, which makes me shut up fast.

"Nah," I say. "Doubt I'd be able to. Never planned on it, anyways. It's fun, but not something I want to do for the rest of my life."

"What do you want to do, though?" she asks.

"Why are you asking me this shit?" I say. "What's it matter?"

"I'm just curious," she says. "That's all."

Oh, well, is that it? That's all? She's asking way too many questions. She's going to make me say something I'll regret.

And... let's just count down, shall we? How long until I do it? Hm...

Three... two... one...

"I want to start my own business," I say. "A club. Something nice. Classy but fun."

"Huh!" she says, like this is some novel, breakthrough idea. I guess it kind of is. "Why?"

Holy fuck. Why? Wow.

"It's stupid," I say. "Don't worry about it."

"It doesn't sound stupid," she says.

"How the fuck can you say that? You don't even know what the idea is."

"I know," she says. "That's why I'd like to hear more about it."

What's up with this reverse psychology bull-shit? I don't like it. I don't say more--I just straight up refuse--but then she cuddles close again and squeezes my hand. I'm not used to this. Apparently this is my tragic flaw, my one true weakness.

"I want to make a place where girls can go and have fun, but they can meet guys who aren't dicks," I say.

"Like you," she adds with a grin.

"Fuck you," I say, but I grin, too.

"You already did," she says.

Wow. Touche, Princess. Slick comeback.

"It's stupid, alright, but I know what it's like. I'm an asshole. I've seen it all before. I know what's up. I can tell if a guy is an asshole or not, so I want to keep those fucks out of the club and get some nice guys in. Not too nice, not those stupid white knight fucks who believe in friend-zone shit. I don't even know if it's possible, though. Was thinking of doing something like a dating site to go along with it. Maybe make a whole set of clubs for different stuff, too."

"Like a private club?" she asks. "So you can have people fill out questions or something like that to see if they fit, with personality tests to go along with it, and then girls can go to the club and know that the guys there aren't going to try and take advantage of them. That sounds neat. I... I don't go to clubs, Ethan, but I know girls who would like that. Sometimes they just want to go out and have fun, but sometimes it's nice to meet people, too, you know? But it's hard, because a lot of the guys..."

"Yeah," I say. "They just want to hook up for the night. I know."

The next question seems pretty fucking obvious, but I don't expect it.

"Do you do that?" she asks.

"Nah," I say. "No point in it."

"I guess not," she says. "Girls are probably all over you. I don't know why."

"Wow. Really? My own sister with the sick burns tonight. I thought I gave you a few good reasons why earlier."

"That can't be the only reason," she says, rolling her eyes.

"Orgasms are a pretty fucking great reason," I say.

"They are nice..." she says, her voice dreamy and cute. Fuck, I love it. "I think they're hoping you'll pick them, though."

"I did pick them," I say.

"That's not what I mean. I meant for more. They're hoping you'll change for them and stay with them. Maybe forever."

"I don't do that," I say.

"I know you don't," she says.

"Good. Glad you get it," I say.

"You just have fun with girls," she says.

This is going somewhere. She's doing it again, isn't she? If this were a court of law, I'm pretty sure there'd be an objection for leading the witness right about now.

"Yeah," I say. "That's what I do."

"I want to have fun with you, Ethan," she says.

"Princess, you and I are going to have a whole lot of fun, don't even worry about it."

"Now?"

Well... fuck. Going to be honest, I'm hard. I've been hard this entire time. Do you know what it's like to have a constant erection? I didn't before recently. It's like a fucking drug. You get light-headed from all the blood being redirected to your cock, and you end up saying stupid shit to your stepsister, and you don't sound like nearly enough of an asshole for a guy who's built his entire reputation around being a bad boy prick.

It's just a really fucking bad situation to be in is what I'm saying.

Ashley lets go of my hand and reaches towards my pants. I've done this before. This isn't my first rodeo. I lift up my hips and give her easy access to unbutton, unzip, and pull down my jeans a little. My cock pops free, bouncing into the air. Yeah, going commando here. Tried to put some underwear on, but it kept pissing me off since my cock refused to go soft. It's a serious problem.

I need a doctor or something. Maybe a nurse. Probably just a blowjob. In my experience, blowjobs usually fix a lot of problems.

Instead of holding my hand, Smarty Pants is holding my cock now. Not nearly as cuddly and sweet, to be honest. I like the way her hand fits around my shaft. Her fingers are a little smaller than average, and it just looks really fucking erotic.

You want to know a surefire way to make a girl blush? Or slap you. One of those. When you first meet her, go up to her, shake her hand like a real gentleman, and then say, "You know, your hand would look amazing holding my cock."

It's a crowd pleaser, for sure.

Except, seriously, Ashley's hand looks amazing holding my cock. No joke. Not even trying to be an asshole right now. I know, right? There's a first time for everything.

She strokes me up and down, slow. She's still watching the movie. I don't know why this is more of a turn on. I'm aroused as fuck, though.

"This is fun," she whispers to me. "No one can see us, but we're out in the open."

"You ever done this before?" I ask.

"No," she says. "Never."

"Never as in... none of it?"

She shakes her head. "It all just um... well, I've had sex, but..."

"Spit in your hand," I tell her.

She freezes. All of her. Even her hand on my cock. I pry her fingers away and hold her hand lightly, like a delicate fucking flower. Yeah, that's right. I'm romantic as fuck.

"Do it," I say. "Trust me."

I bring her hand up to her mouth and hold it beneath her chin. She just kind of... drools? It's not spitting at all. It's like a slip of saliva crawling down her tongue and into her palm.

"Princess, I get it. You're not the kind of girl who does this shit. But we're going to do it, alright? Unless you want to stop right now," I say. "Do you?"

She shakes her head, no. "It's just weird," she says.

"It's not weird. It's sexy as fuck. Now, seriously, just go all out. Not too crazy. Don't want to spit everywhere. But do it like you mean it."

She nods. This is serious. And funny. She's treating this like I'm some teacher and she's a student sitting in a classroom. Which... well, fuck, I guess it's kind of true. This is some next level calculus, isn't it? Let me write out the equation for you. I know it well

SPIT + HAND + COCK = HANDJOB

The tricky part is solving for O. Don't worry, I plan on showing Ashley exactly how it's done.

She does it. She spits. It's good, too. I can't stop staring at her. There's a little slip of saliva creeping from her lip to her palm, just hovering there. I want to see that same thing later, but from her lip to my cock when she's taking a break from giving me head.

My cock twitches in anticipation at what's coming next. I guide her hand back to my shaft, wrap her fingers around it again, and help her with the first few strokes.

"See?" I say. "Yeah, I can see how maybe it seems gross at first, but trust me, it's sexy. You just have to own it. Don't think about it, don't worry about it, just make it your thing. Trust me, it's an instant turn on."

"You were already turned on, though," she says with a smirk.

"Yeah? And now I'm turned on even more."

"More?" she asks.

"Princess, I've been waiting hours to do something like this with you."

"What does that mean?" she asks.

What's that mean? I laugh. "Sometimes it's nice to go slow. Other times it's good to go fast. You want to see me cum? Just go fast right now. It won't take long, I promise."

"Can I?" she asks, her eyes lighting up. "Um... you won't be mad? I've never seen it before. When a guy cums, I mean. I'd like to."

I gesture towards my cock with a flourish, like a gentleman opening a door for a lady. I'm not a fucking gentleman, and this lady just spit in her hand so she can use it as lube to give me a handjob, so...

"Yeah, by all means, have at it."

She does. Slow at first, gaining confidence, and then she's full on into it. Shit. I squeeze my ass against the seat, tensing my thighs. I'm not that bad at this. I can hold off a little, make it exciting for her.

"Ethan, I want to see it. Tell me when you're going to, alright?" she asks.

Yeah, well, fuck. Do you know how sexy those words are? Really sexy. I can't even begin to tell you. This is about her, not me. This has always been about her, not me. I've been waiting for hours to cum, and I kind of thought I was going to do it deep inside her gorgeous pussy, but whatever works, right?

"Slow down a little, Princess," I say. "Just slow down for five seconds, then speed up again, back and forth like that, alright?"

"Slow for five, then fast for five, and slow again?" she asks.

"Yeah, just like that."

She slows down. Aw yeah. Smooth and slick, I can see my cock glistening with a mix of my precum and her spit. Then fast. The shine glimmers in the moonlight, a combination of the speed of her strokes and the shimmer of the lubrication.

Slow. Fast. Yeah. That's it. Slow again.

"Fast," I say. "Don't stop."

She listens. She does exactly what I say. It's fucking intoxicating, that's what it is. My body tightens and my balls prepare to unleash my pent up arousal. Little Miss Perfect leans down to watch. If my eyes weren't glazed over in lust, I'd probably warn her to back up right about now, but uh... yeah...

I'm done. I cum. She keeps stroking me and I squirm from the sensation. My seed shoots up, fierce and hard. My cock was kind of expecting pussy to lambaste, but it's just got open air, so the force is more than excessive. Mostly it just shoots up, then splashes back down. Mostly.

She's close. Watching. One jet of cum hits her cheek near her lips. That one's going to stick. There's no coming down from that. She gasps and flinches, backing up, then she starts to laugh.

She's fucking laughing. And stroking my cock. I'm still coming. Shit, it's sensitive. Too much. But she's not stopping. Holy fuck, that's nice. Usually I make them stop right now, but I'm not sure if I want her to or not. I kind of want to go again. Is that normal? Fuck if I know.

She stops eventually. My cream's all over her fingers and some is on the corner of her lip. I stare at her, brow furrowed.

"That's what you get," I say. "You can't get too close or something like that's going to happen."

And you know what? You know what she does?

She pokes out her tongue and licks her lips. Not just her lips, but to the side, towards my cum. Just laps that shit up. Pulls her tongue back in, wrinkles her nose. She looks real contemplative right now, like she's thinking about something deep and meaningful.

"You taste good, Ethan," she says. Then she brings her hand to her mouth and starts licking my cum from her fingers. "Wow."

Instant erection. I thought I just came, but now I don't even know what's real or not. Maybe this is all a dream. I'm going to wake up and none of this will have happened.

I dive for her. I'm done. This is over. Movie? Where the fuck are we? I don't fucking care. I grab her pants, practically rip the button off, slam down the zipper, and pull her jeans down her legs. Not all the way. I don't fucking care if they're off or not. They just need to be off enough for me to ram my cock inside her.

She laughs and squirms and wriggles away from me, but I'm not going to deal with that. Oh no, not now, Princess.

"Ethan!" she shrieks, but it's hushed. We're still at the drive-in, and I'm pretty sure she realizes that.

"Come here, Princess," I say, smooth. "Sit in my lap."

She comes. She sits. She's facing forward, looking at the movie screen, and I am, too. My cock throbs between her thighs.

"Stand up a little," I say. When she does, I pull her panties to the side, then pull her back down.

Right on my cock. Right fucking on it.

She's wet. Wetter than wet. Yeah, good. I'm glad I'm not the only one aroused by this situation.

As soon as she sinks down on me and I fill her completely, she lets out a loud gasp. "Oh my God," she says. "Ethan, we're..."

"I know where we are," I say. "And I don't fucking care."

"It's so *wrong*," she says. Is that... holy fuck, she's talking dirty to me, isn't she? Not very well. We can work on that.

"You want it," I tell her.

"Ethan, you're my stepbrother!"

I didn't know how much of a turn on that was until she says it while I'm balls deep inside her, my cock twitching and throbbing and covered with cum from when she gave me a handjob. It's just so fucking... taboo. Holy fuck. I probably should have realized this before now, but yeah, whatever. It's not even about that, but at the moment she's apparently decided to make it a little about that.

I wrap my hand around her stomach and pull her close. My other hand sneaks up her shirt and starts fondling her breast. She grinds against my lap, moving exactly how I want her to.

"I've only ever had sex in the regular position," she says. "I've never been on top like this."

"How do you like it?" I ask.

"I... can you touch me? My..."

"Say it, Princess. Say it and I'll do whatever you want."

"Ethan, can you... can you rub my clit with your fingers? Beneath my panties?"

"Say it again," I tell her. "Say it like you mean it. Say it like you'll die if I don't do it."

"Brother, I need you!" she says, gasping out the words. "I need you to rub my clit. I want you to make me cum on your cock. I want you to cum inside me, too. I want it so bad."

Holy... what the fuck? Where did that come from? It's like she's been...

Brother? Fucking hell. That's some sick shit. I don't know why this turns me on. I guess it doesn't help that she's literally never called me this before, not once. It's new and strange and I don't know how I feel about it. I'm going to have to have a talk with her about this later.

She's my stepsister, I remind myself. It's not actually wrong. I mean, it's not like this is the best thing in the world. I'm not going to tell anyone about it. But it's not actually fucked up, you know? It's technically perfectly legal...

I don't even know how. The way my cock feels inside her pussy... something this good should definitely be illegal.

I slip my hand under the waistband of her panties and tease and rub at her clit. Or, that's what I planned on doing, but as soon as I touch her, her back arches hard and she starts to tremble and shake. Too hard? Too rough? I ease up a little, but she grabs my hand and pulls it back.

"No no no no please," she hisses, frantic.

I'm confused for a second, but then I realize it.

Holy fucking shit, this girl is responsive as fuck. I guess I wasn't the only one waiting for this. I rub slow, but steady, keeping it up, and yeah... she's cumming. I feel her grip and squeeze against my cock, her slick arousal getting even wetter. Her panties, my cock, and my fingers are soaked now.

She's not grinding anymore. It's fine, no big deal. My cock isn't going soft anytime soon. I'm pretty sure I could stand up right now and keep her in the air just with the strength of my erection. No hands necessary.

She gasps and pants and starts to breathe faster, then she slumps against me, coming down from her sexual high. I rub her clit lightly still, keeping her peaked and interested. I'm pretty sure it's not going to take much...

"Can you do it again?" she asks. "Not me. You, I mean. Can you? Inside me?"

"Yeah," I say, grinning. "Your wish is my command, Princess."

Were we watching a movie? Two movies? Double feature, right? We're at a drive-in movie theatre. Good thing the back windows are tinted. It's dark, anyways. Probably doesn't matter. The car might be rocking. That's never a good thing. I don't fucking care. A world-destroying meteor could crash down right next to us, destroying everything but our car, and I wouldn't notice.

I think I'm in love with this girl. With her pussy, that is. Don't get the wrong fucking idea. This is Ashley we're talking about. My stepsister.

She deserves someone better than me. She'll find him some day.

# 6 - *Ashley*

I'M SO TIRED. I can't believe we did that, either. I never would have done that with anyone else. I don't think I would have.

My sex life up until now has been... adequate. I think that's the best word to describe it.

What's sex, really? Technically it's a process by which a male and female of the same species can create new life. In which case, I suppose my sex hasn't even been adequate, scientifically speaking. And I'm very thankful for that. I don't want to have a baby, at least not now. Later, when I'm settled, when I've found someone I love, who I want to marry, and...

But sex can be fun, too, can't it? I suppose it's technically not necessary, at least as far as science and biology are concerned, but I think it's nice when it is. And in that case, my sex life has also been lackluster. It's felt... good. When I've had sex, it does feel good.

But it's never felt like anything compared to the way Ethan makes me feel. It's more than the sex, too. A lot more.

Oh God! I can't believe I said some of what I said, too. Brother? I mean, technically he's my stepbrother, and it's not completely out of the ordinary for me to call him brother. He calls my mom "Mom" and I call his dad "Dad" and it was weird at first and we didn't do that, but we've lived together for a few years now and it's coming more natural.

I've never called him that before, though. I don't think I'm good at dirty talk, but when Ethan had me spit in my hand to give him a handjob, um... I just wanted to be dirtier? I wanted to have fun, like he says we're doing. And we are having fun, but...

I don't know. Maybe that was too much. Maybe I went too far. Maybe it was gross? When I think about it now, it is kind of gross. Except Ethan's cock grew even harder inside me as soon as I said it, too.

Maybe it's alright to say some things during sex when you know you wouldn't say them otherwise. Is that it? It makes a little sense, in a strange way. I'll ask him later and if he didn't like it I'll apologize.

I'm just so tired right now, though. We're home again. I don't know how Ethan can drive after what we did, but he managed to do it. Are we going to have sex? Again?

He parks in the garage and turns off the car. As soon as he steps out of the car, the interior garage light flips on. I go to open my own door and try to step out, to walk inside, but it's difficult.

Silent, saying nothing, Ethan comes around to my side of the car. He opens the door for me. I hold out my hand to take his so he can help me up, but his hand isn't there. Not exactly.

He lifts me up, sliding one arm behind my back. His other arm cradles beneath my legs. Gently, carefully, he pulls me up and out of the car, carrying me in his arms. I don't say anything. I'm too tired to. I rest my head against his chest and close my eyes and listen to the sound of his heart and his breathing and his soft steps as we walk through the garage.

He'll put me down once we get inside, I'm sure. Except he doesn't.

While still carrying me, he types in the key code on the numpad to open the house door, then twists the knob to let us inside, and also somehow manages to close the door behind us. Then, still holding me tight, he walks through the halls of the first floor, heading to the staircase. And up. Up. Up. His feet thud against the carpeted steps, and I count them silently in my head, like slumbering sheep.

When we get to the top of the stairs, I open my eyes a little. Where are we going? To my bedroom, or...?

No. To his. He carries me down the hall to his room. The door is already open, since he never bothered to close it before we left. He flicks on the light and brings me to his bed, placing me gently on top of the covers.

I smile at him. "Can I sleep in here with you tonight?" I ask.

"Yeah," he says. "I'll get you out of your clothes."

"I... Ethan, I don't know if I can have sex again today," I say.

He laughs. "Nah, it's fine. Me either. You tired me out, Princess."

"Really?" I ask. That sounds impressive. I think he must be lying, but it's not a bad lie. It's a fun one.

"Really," he says.

He pulls off my shoes, one by one, and tosses them to the floor. Then my socks along with them. He moves to unbutton my pants, too.

"Ethan, can we cuddle?"

He hesitates before answering, pulling my jeans down my legs, leaving me almost bare. His fingers wrap into the waistband of my panties before he says, "Why do you want to do that, Princess?"

"They always leave," I say. It hurts. I never realized how much it hurts until now. "No one ever stays the night with me. Not even..."

Not even Jake. I don't want to think about Jake. I never want to think about him again. I...

I want to think about Ethan. I know I shouldn't, but I want to. Even if it's just a week, that's fine. It's...

I don't know if it's fine.

"They're stupid," he says. "Whoever it is, they're fucking stupid. Yeah, I'll cuddle with you, Princess."

"I don't know how to," I say. "That sounds dumb, huh?"

"Nah," he says, smiling. He lifts me up a little and pulls off my shirt. "I don't know how to, either. We'll figure it out."

Oh...

He unclasps my bra, leaving me completely naked now. I close my eyes, but I can hear him undressing beside me. I imagine Ethan naked in my mind, even if I could simply open my eyes and see him naked. First his shoes, then his pants. He didn't wear underwear tonight. I wonder if he does that often? Finally he pulls his shirt up and over his head. Then he...

"Come on," he says. "Stand up for a second. Need to lift the covers up."

I keep my eyes closed, but I move into his arms when he helps me up and off the bed. We're both naked, standing close. I wrap my arms around him and nuzzle my cheek against his chest, and he holds me tight with one arm while sweeping back the blankets with the other. When he's done, he swoops me into his arms and lays me in bed. Shortly after, he follows.

Ethan reaches above his head and flicks a switch, covering us in darkness. Everything is black. It's almost midnight now. The double feature movies run late, but that's part of what I like about them. I lay on my back in bed next to Ethan, who is laying the same way. There's blankets over us now, keeping us close and warm.

Slowly, unsure, I roll to the side and drape my arm over his chest. I put my head partway on his shoulder and the pillow. He curls his arm around me, loose at first, but after a second he squeezes me tighter. His confidence makes me bold. I lift up my leg and wrap it around his, my knee resting near his hip, my thigh close to the core of his body.

Ethan kisses the top of my head and I nuzzle even closer to him.

"You comfortable?" he asks.

"Mhm," I murmur.

"Good," he says. "Let's get some sleep."

"What about tomorrow?" I ask.

"What about it?" he says.

"Will you still be here?"

"Yeah," he says. After a short pause, he adds, "I'll always be here, Ashley."

"Always?" I ask.

He chuckles. "Yeah, where do you think I'm going to go? I live here too, remember?"

Oh... right...

I knew that.

It's just...

"G'night, Ethan," I say, kissing his bare chest. He feels warm and soft beneath me. I like cuddling.

"G'night," he says.

# 7 - Ethan

WHAT THE FUCK? What are you even doing here?

I'm trying to sleep.

Do you think you can read into my innermost thoughts, my secret feelings, and figure something out? Nah, probably not. Whatever. You want to see what I dream about? Alright then, have at it.

I guess you want me to say that I've never slept this well before, but you're wrong. The best night's sleep I ever had was after my first night of double practice sessions for football during my freshman year of high school. Six hours of practice split between three hour sessions, one in the morning, then a couple hours of break, and another in the afternoon.

Up until then, practice for football was kind of easy. Just junior league level shit, nothing crazy or intense. In high school you go hard, though. There's a lot going on, a lot to learn, and you need to actually get into shape. I thought I was doing pretty well for myself before that, but apparently not. Your muscles burn for days until you finally manage to break through the aches and stiffness from doing something you've never done before.

The night after my first day of that was my best night's sleep ever. I still remember what I dreamed about. Is it weird to dream about a dream you had before? I don't know. Who cares?

First day of high school double sessions was also the beginning of cheerleader practice. They were a little pickier about who they allowed on the squad, so there was actual training and tryouts going on. For football, at least at the high school level, they basically just let anyone on the team. You either quit because you can't move anymore and you're too lazy to keep trying, or you stick it out. You might not play a lot, but it's still fun to fuck around during practice.

Not everyone's a hero. Not everyone has to be in the spotlight. Sounds fucked up coming from me, I know. It's true, though. I like everyone I play with, whether they're third string and never actually play during a game, or they're guarding me as I move back to make a game winning pass. They all went through the same shit I did, they survived, and they kept going. For that, they have my respect.

Cheerleaders don't have time for that many extra girls on the squad, though, so they do it differently. Whatever. What do I care? I'm not a cheerleader. Never wanted to be one, either. They can do what they want.

The thing is, Ashley was trying out that year. Never thought of her as the cheerleader type, but I could definitely get used to seeing her in those short skirts. I kept glancing over during practice to see what was going on with her, and she looked like she was doing alright. Struggling a little, but whatever. Everyone has to start somewhere, right? I admit she's not the most athletic girl in the world, but I feel like she has potential if you give her a chance.

So... well... yeah, my dreams that night consisted of the heavy sleep of someone who is drop dead tired from exertion, none of their muscles able to do much more than almost flex, and thinking about what it'd be like to throw a game winning touchdown, and have one of the cheerleaders run out on the field, jump into my arms, wrap her legs around my waist, and just make out with me right there.

In my mind, the cheerleader may or may not have been Ashley. That was before all this crazy shit happened. Don't get any ideas. She still wore glasses then, and maybe our parents were dating but they never told us. I didn't know she was going to be my stepsister some day. I didn't know we'd end up in this screwed up "with benefits" situation that we're in now.

I wish I'd known. Maybe it would have made all this easier. Probably not. Oh well.

She never came back after that, though. Just left. I don't know what happened. I guess I've always kind of wondered, but it's none of my business. Maybe she hated it.

It would have been nice, though. Not my dream, because what the fuck, what do I care about that? I mean, yeah, that would have been nice, too, but...

Just would have been nice seeing her on the sidelines, cheering. I don't know why. Don't ask me that. It's complicated. Confusing as fuck, even to me.

Tonight is different. It's nice, but in a different way.

I wake up in the middle of the night and there's some cuddly fucking teddy bear on me or something? When I open my eyes, I see her. Her hair's covering her face a little, but she's got her head on my shoulder, cheek cradled against my neck. One of her arms clings to me tight, and she has her leg wrapped around me, too.

Also, she's naked. Yeah, that's right. Of course she is, since I stripped her down before we got into bed. I'm naked, too. And hard as fuck. She moves a little in her sleep and her leg shifts closer to me, rubbing against my cock. I twitch uncontrollably.

This isn't supposed to be erotic. She's sleeping for fuck's sake!

I guess it's not that it's erotic, it's just that I can't help it. I can't stop thinking about her. I don't know why, I just can't.

I have one arm tight around her, under her head, holding her close. I move my other hand to grab her leg and pull her even closer to me. She opens her mouth and yawns slightly, then mumbles in her sleep. I wonder what she's dreaming about? You think it's about me? That'd be nice, huh?

I caress my fingers up her thigh to the center of her body, then nearer to her ass. I hold her there, squeezing slightly.

This week is supposed to be about her. About making her feel better. More confident. I know that, but I can't help wanting to explore every inch of her body, too. I want to touch her all over, to figure her out, to map her entire fucking existence in my mind so I'll never forget it. I stretch my fingers lower, reaching around and behind her, until my fingertips tease at the entrance to her sex.

Just a little. I just want to fucking touch her. I'm not going to do anything weird or twisted. Get the fuck out of here. I hold her like that and she shivers and trembles in my arms, then clings tighter and closer to me. I move my hand away slightly and rub up and down her thigh, calming and smooth.

I kiss her. Her forehead. Yeah, fuck you, I kiss her forehead. She wrinkles her nose a little, probably because her hair is in her face, tickling her. I kiss her nose, too. Then her eye, her cheek. I crane my neck up and to the side until I can kiss her on the lips, too. She pouts her lips a little, wrinkling her nose, then she kisses in her sleep. Not a real kiss, nothing crazy and passionate and full of lust, but it's sweet and cute and nice.

I love it. I kiss her again and just lay like that with her in my arms. She keeps kissing, and we do a back and forth thing. My lips, her lips, mine again.

I whisper something into her ear before closing my eyes again. You want to know what I whisper? Fuck off, I've already told you more than enough. Get out of my head.

# *8 - Ashley*

OHHHHHHHHH...

So *this* is what it's like? To wake up next to someone, cuddled in their arms, soft and warm and comfortable? Yes, apparently so.

I knew I would know how it felt one day. I've always thought about it, maybe even daydreamed about it a little bit now and again. Or a lot. I just... I thought maybe it was something for everyone else. Not for me. It was for people who were...

Better. Better than me.

Except now I can feel it, too. I admit that I never thought I'd first experience something like this with Ethan, with my stepbrother, but now that it has, I'm kind of glad. I feel more comfortable in a lot of ways. Safer. Because I've lived in this house for years. I've been in this room before, even though we've never really spent much time alone together like this before now. I've seen Ethan in the halls. I've eaten with him; breakfast, lunch, and dinner. I sleep right down the hall from him, too. I can get up, step outside his room, walk to mine, and find all of my things.

It's kind of like we've skipped a step. Sort of. Um...

Because you know how people start dating, and then eventually they move in together, and they can see each other all the time? I know that Ethan and I aren't dating, but we've already moved in together, sort of. We've already seen each other all the time. Even before now I used to see him almost every day during school. Sometimes he was in the same classes as me, but otherwise I'd see him at lunch or recess or after school.

It just makes me feel more comfortable, that's all. Like I can be more of myself around him, even though I've found it difficult to really open up to him before this. To be fair, he hasn't exactly opened up to me, either.

That's alright. After this, things will change. I hope. For the better. Because...

I can feel him against my leg, and it makes me giggle. He's got an erection? In his sleep? I've heard about this, but never seen it firsthand. I reach down his chest, feeling every line of his muscular abs, then a little lower still, to...

His cock. Yesss...

I touch it. Just a little. He twitches, and I grin. I touch him more, wrapping my fingers around him while he sleeps. He squirms in bed then bucks his hips up slightly humping my hand and the air and the blanket above him. Oh no. Is he going to wake up? What if I go slowly?

This... um... feels very wrong, but...

I stroke him very very slowly in my hands, up, then down. He grows even harder, which is almost startling. He's almost too sexual, but it's fascinating in an intoxicating sort of way. I don't know how he does it. I stroke him a couple more times in his sleep and...

No. Oh no. Really? Oh my God, what have I done? Ethan's cock starts twitching and spasming uncontrollably even after I stop, but my fingers are still wrapped around his cock, and um... soon I have his cum on them, too. I definitely didn't mean to do that. Apparently he's very sensitive in his sleep? Or he's been working himself up in a dream for awhile now. I wonder what he's dreaming about?

A part of me hopes it's me. I hope he's dreaming about me. I don't know why. I know it's wrong, but I hope he thinks about me. I hope he...

I carefully slip away from him, trying not to wake him. I hold the blankets up so I can slide my hand free and not make a mess on his sheets with my now cum-covered hand. It's um... well, huh! I didn't even know something like that could happen. Now I know, right? I guess it's a good thing to have found out, though I'm not sure when I'll ever be able to put this new knowledge to use. Probably never, but that's alright.

Ethan opens his mouth and yawns, then reaches towards me, but I slip away quick. I place a pillow in his arms instead and he wraps around it, hugging it tight. Like he's hugging me. I wonder if that's what he means to do?

No, that's stupid. He doesn't mean to do anything. He's asleep.

I accidentally lick my hand. Which is to say I just don't realize what I'm doing until I stop to think about it, but I'm definitely licking Ethan's cum off my hand. To be fair, I kind of like it. It tastes good. A little sweet. I've heard that this doesn't taste good, but I don't have any other experience to measure it by, and Ethan's tastes good, so I'll just go with that. I should probably be getting a tissue or going to the bathroom to clean this off, but...

Nope! I can do what I want!

I lick the rest off, grinning to myself. My little secret, right? Mhm.

And now to... what?

I'm going to make him breakfast, I decide. Ethan made me breakfast, and now I'll make him breakfast. My legs are sore, though. And more. I feel like I've used muscles I've never used before, some of which are decidedly centered on the core of my body. Um... inside me... and yes, I know there are muscles there, but it's just weird to have a constant, aching reminder that maybe they've recently had quite an extensive workout.

It's fun, though. A sore, sexy fun. I like it, because it reminds me of Ethan and what we did together. And I liked that, so...

I find my panties from the night before and slip them on, then I grab Ethan's t-shirt. It's too big for me, but I put it on anyways. Just those two things, my panties and his shirt. It's not like there's anyone else here, so what does it matter, right?

I sneak out of his room, then skip down the hall to the stairs. Every step I take sends a tingling ache through my body, a light reminder of exactly what Ethan and I were doing last night. Mmm...

When I get downstairs, I head to the kitchen, and...

What to make, what to make. Hm...? Ethan likes omelets. Do we have spinach and feta cheese? I check the fridge quick and, yes, we do! Plus tomatoes and hunks of chicken breast, which, if you ask me, sounds like the perfect ingredients to make a Greek-style omelet. I take all of those out, along with the eggs, and put them on the counter.

Maybe French toast, too? Ethan's dad buys this special sort of thick bread that's nice as either French toast or garlic bread slices, but we don't always have it, so I check and... yes! We do. That sounds nice, doesn't it?

I start to crack eggs to make the French toast glaze, mix mix swirl, a woman on a mission. That's me. Everything is going well, but then the buzzer sounds for the front gates. I check the clock and it's still early, so it's probably just the mailman delivering a package. I skip to the front door and click the button to open the gates for him, then head back to the kitchen. He'll probably just leave the package unless I have to...

The doorbell rings. Ugh. Yup, have to sign for the package. Oh well.

I don't usually walk around the house half naked, so I kind of belatedly realize what I must look like, but Ethan's shirt is long and it covers everything important, so I guess it's fine. My thighs are half revealed, and the rest of my legs are bare, but other than that no one can really see much. I open the door to sign for the package and...

Well, that's not a package, now is it? I recognize the boy standing on our front stoop. One of Ethan's friends. He looks indifferent at first, but when he sees me standing there, his eyes widen and he perks up, then smiles.

"Hey," he says.

"Um... hello," I say.

"Ethan here?" he asks.

"He's sleeping," I say.

"Ah, cool, cool. He told me to come by sometime this week, so figured I'd stop over."

"Oh." I guess? What can I really say to that? "I can go get him if you want?"

"Nah, it's cool. Mind if I come in and wait for him to wake up?"

I suppose not? I don't know. I'm not sure why Ethan wants him to come over, to be honest. Maybe it's important? I shrug and step aside and he steps inside.

"Johnny," he says, holding out his hand in greeting.

"Ashley," I say, taking his hand, intending to shake it. He pulls it up to his lips and kisses the back of my hand instead, though.

I freeze. Mostly because this is strange. I guess it's nice? Chivalrous? It just makes me uncomfortable, that's all. Probably mostly because of what I'm wearing.

I pull my hand back and try not to stammer. "Ummm... well, you can just wait around, I guess. Ethan will probably be up soon. I'm just making breakfast."

"Yeah, that's cool," Johnny says. "I'm not in a hurry."

I close the door and lock it, then hurry back to the safety of the kitchen. The living room is further down the hall, easy to find and see, and that's definitely where he'll go wait for Ethan, so I can just stay in here, make breakfast, and...

No, apparently not. Johnny stands in the doorway of the kitchen, watching me. I don't realize it at first because I'm busy whisking eggs to make omelets, but then when I turn around, I nearly jump out of my skin. The whisk clatters to the ground, but I manage not to tip the bowl over, too.

When I bend down to pick up the whisk, I realize that Ethan's shirt is very loose on me and I didn't bother putting my bra on. Looking up, I see Johnny looking down, leering at me, a wicked grin on his face. He steps into the kitchen, moving closer to me. Too close. I don't like this. I back away from him, trying to put distance between us, but he doesn't take the hint.

"You look like you could use some help," he says, putting one hand on my hip.

I stiffen and freeze. I'm trapped, by his body and the counter in front of me. He's standing behind me, cornering me with his hand on my hip, his other arm leaning against the counter, looming over my shoulder. His fingers grab at the cloth of my shirt and pull it up a little until he can slide his hand underneath. Now he's touching me directly, his palm against my bare side, the edge of his fingers resting against my panties.

"What are you making?" he asks.

I shiver, teeth chattering, but somehow manage to say, "Ummmm... omelets... and French toast..."

"You're shivering," he says, amused. "You cold, babe? Maybe you should take a break. I can help keep you warm. Give me something to do while I wait, right? You want to be a good host and show me to a room where we can have some private time together?"

He asks me this, but it's obvious he doesn't actually want me to answer him. He's already pulling me away from the counter, pulling me closer to him, his hand creeping up my stomach, his other hand moving to my side, to my panties. He tries to reach under the waistband of my panties just as he moves his hand up to the under-side of my breasts, and I... I freeze... I... this has never... um... what do I...

I feel a sharp jerk, and then nothing. I'm standing alone again, no one's touching me. I stumble and fall towards the counter. My hands clap against the countertop and I hold myself up, regaining my balance, then spin around because...

It's Ethan. My stepbrother. He must have grabbed Johnny and pulled him away from me. They're facing each other now. Sort of. It's a fraction of a second. Everything happens so fast. Ethan's holding Johnny's shirt collar tight in his hands, keeping him at arm's length, then he punches him.

As easy as that. Simple. Nothing to it. Ethan winds back and slams his fist into Johnny's jaw with an audible slap of knuckle against cheek, a sickening crack sound following soon after.

"Man, what are you..." Johnny starts to say, his words coming out slurred and broken.

Ethan pulls him back up, not letting him fall, then he twists him around and shoves him to the entrance of the kitchen. Johnny slips on the smooth tile floors and falls face first against the hallway rug.

"That's my fucking sister, you prick!" Ethan shouts at him. "What the fuck are you doing? Get the fuck out of here!"

"Man, I was just being friendly. What the fuck? She's the one that opened the door half naked. It's not my fault."

Ethan glares at him. I feel like maybe he's going to kill him. I don't know why. It's silly. Ethan won't kill someone, will he? Um... I didn't think so before, but now I'm not so sure. I rush over and cling to Ethan's back, wrapping my arms around him.

"Please stop?" I whisper. "I'm fine, I just..."

I'm not fine. I'm shaking. I'm scared. Doubly scared. I'm scared of what Johnny was doing, but I'm also scared of what Ethan might do to him because of that.

"You ever touch her again, I'll fucking kill you," Ethan says, practically spitting on him. "I don't fucking care if she opens the door naked. Got it? That doesn't give you the right to do anything, you stupid fuck."

"Whatever, man," Johnny says. "You asked me to come over so I came over. Didn't mean to fuck with your sister. I thought she wanted it."

"She doesn't. Now get out."

There might have been more to it, but I'm not sure. Ethan "escorts" Johnny out while I stay in the kitchen. My knees shake and I have to hold onto the counter to keep myself from crashing to the ground in a wobbly, trembling mess. A few minutes later Ethan comes back and he sees me like that, scared, shaking.

"Ohhh, Princess," he says. He sounds hurt. Why is he hurt? I'm the one who...

Is that why he's hurt? It makes my heart melt. I want to think that's the real reason, but I'm not sure.

He comes to my side and puts his arm around me. "Come on, let's go sit down, alright?"

I nod and go with him when he starts to walk. We move slow, careful. I can barely keep my footing, but Ethan holds me tight, never letting me go. We head to the sunroom overlooking the pool, then sit in one of the benches there. It's nice out, and the glass walls of the room magnify the heat of the sun, making it cozy and warm in here.

Ethan sits on the bench and pulls me down with him. I curl close to him, hovering against him. He's so warm and soft and this room is warmer still. I like it a lot.

"I don't know what happened," I say quietly, whispering into his ear. "Ethan, I just... I thought he was the mailman delivering a package, so I went to the door without thinking, and then... I was just going to make us breakfast. I didn't know he was coming and I don't know why he did that."

"Because he's a stupid fucking prick," Ethan says. "A stupid fucking prick who thinks any girl without pants on his just asking to fuck."

"I didn't, though," I say. "I didn't ask him to do that. I didn't want him to. I..." Oh no. I start to cry.

"You don't think I did, do you? You believe me, right?"

Ethan chokes up, startled. "Princess, don't cry. Of course I believe you. Ashley, I know you'd never do that."

"But I... I..." I did. I have. Yesterday. With him. I... "What about..."

I think he realizes it. I think he must. He knows what I'm about to say, about us, about...

"It's different," he says. "Yeah, fuck, maybe we shouldn't be doing it, either, but it's different. I wouldn't do anything unless you wanted me to. You know that, right? You can tell me to stop any time and I will. Promise me you'll tell me if you want me to stop, alright?"

I nod fast, tears dripping down my cheek and splashing against his chest. He doesn't have a shirt on, I realize. He's wearing pants, but not a shirt. I have his shirt, but no pants. I guess that makes us a pair? The thought makes me laugh a little, but then I'm crying still, and it must look ugly and wretched to laugh and cry at the same time.

That's me. That's how I've always been. No one's ever wanted to be with me. No one.

Ethan has. He's with me right now.

For a week. That's it. Does that even count?

"Do you think we should stop?" I ask. "I mean, do you think we should stop this? Ethan, I don't think what we're doing is good. I don't think we're supposed to do this."

"What do you want?" he asks. "You tell me what you want, Princess. Do you want to stop? We can if you want."

"Am I forcing you?" I ask. "Is it like that for you? Do you want to or do you feel bad and that's why?"

"Nah," he says, smiling softly. He kisses my cheek, kisses away my tears. I cuddle closer to him, nuzzling against his lips. "It's not like that, Princess. I'll stop if you want to stop, but if you want to go, well... fuck, I'm ready."

I laugh, remembering this morning. "I know," I say. "I can tell. Um... did you feel weird when you woke up?"

He scrunches up his brow, looking at me funny. "Huh?"

"Um... when I woke up, you were... you... you had an erection, and um... I just kind of wanted to touch it. I didn't know guys actually had erections in their sleep. So I did. But then I started doing a little more and then..."

"That was you?" he asks, smirking. "Fuck, I thought I had a wet dream or something. Haven't had one of those in years, though, so it was a little weird."

"Um, nope, that was me," I say, shy. "I didn't mean to. It was an accident."

"It's cool," he says. "Surprised me when I woke up, but now that you've told me, it's pretty sexy."

"Sexy?" I ask. "Really?"

"Yeah, sexy as fuck. God, Ashley, when I saw you wrap your hand around my cock last night, I almost fucking exploded. Do you even know how much you turn me on?"

I laugh a little and wriggle in his arms, but he pulls me close, keeping me tight to him. "Are you being serious?" I ask.

"Yeah, super serious," he says. "Never been more serious in my life."

"Other girls probably turn you on more, though," I say. "I'm just kind of average."

"Nah," he says. "Listen, I know you're just going to think I say this to every girl, but I don't. I'm saying it to you right now, and I mean it. It's just you, Princess. I've never been with anyone sexier than you. I've never been with anyone who's turned me on more than you have. Never."

"Liar..." I say, mumbling.

"You want me to prove it?" he asks, grinning with devilish intent.

One of his hands moves to cup my breast, and my nipple stiffens immediately upon contact. He kneads and massages my breast, gently twisting and tweaking my nipple between his fingers over my shirt.

"I..."

I do. And yet...

"I like when you touch me like that," I say, whispering. "But Ethan, I'm really sore."

He stops, confused, then smirks at me. "You're sore? Like sex sore? Your legs?"

"And inside," I say. "There's muscles in there, too, you know? I didn't realize how much of a workout they got, but I guess it makes sense."

"Wow," he says with a grin so big it could split his face in two. "Didn't realize I was that good."

"Well, I don't know for sure, but I think you are," I tell him, grinning, too. "Also, um... you're a little big."

"A little big?" he asks. "Please, can you stroke my ego some more, Princess?"

I could, I think. I could tell him how much I appreciate him caring for me, for taking care of me. I could say that I love the fact that he's patient and kind to me, that he's gentle when I need someone to be gentle to me, but he knows when to be a little rough, too. I could tell him that I thought I'd regret this forever when I woke up that morning after our accidental night together, but after spending the entire day with him after that, that I don't regret it at all.

I could tell him that the only thing I'll regret about this is that we only have a week together. Except I can never tell him that. I need to stop. I need to understand that this is a temporary situation and that I'll never have it ever again, because no matter what, it won't work out, whether I want it to or not.

And this is Ethan Colton we're talking about. I can't change him. I know this, but it doesn't stop me from hoping and wishing and wanting...

"Can I ask you something?" I ask.

"Yeah, anything," he says.

"Can we not have sex today?"

"No sex," he says, nodding. "Got it."

"But..."

"But?" he asks. "But what?"

"You can say no if you want, but maybe we can still spend the day together and have fun?" I ask.

"Nah, no way," he says. I knew it was too much to ask for. Then he adds, "Why would you want to hang out with me? I'm just an arrogant prick."

I smile and roll my eyes at him. "Shut up. I don't think you are."

"You don't know me that well then, Princess," he says, grinning. Quick and fleeting, he kisses me on the nose. "Yeah, I'll spend the day with you. Sounds fun. What do you want to do?"

"Do you have any plans or anything? Like with um...?"

"Nah, that stupid fuck is gone. I texted him before you came back from college. Thought it'd be nice to have someone to hang out with this summer, but I found someone better. I don't want to ever see that asshole again."

"Oh," I say. "Who did you find?"

"Are you serious?" he asks, looking confused.

"Um... yes?"

"I thought you were smart, Ashley. I really thought you were smart. Now I'm not so sure."

"I don't... no really, who is... wait, me? No, that's not it, is it?"

He pulls me close into a tight embrace, but this one is different. It's intimate, but it feels different, too. It's closer, more... like he really is my brother now? Like we're actually a family, even if we aren't really. It's like...

"Yeah, you're pretty cool for a Smarty Pants Goodie Two Shoe Little Miss Perfect Princess," he says. "You're growing on me, Ashley. I could get used to this."

"Do you want to make breakfast with me? I was going to try and make it before you woke up, but um... you're awake now. I didn't start cooking yet, but everything's ready."

"Yeah, what are we having?"

"I was going to make omelets. Greek-style ones, with tomatoes and feta cheese and spinach and grilled chicken breast. And then French toast."

"Oooh," Ethan says, his eyes lighting up. "We got any Greek yogurt? Plain? Would go good on top of the omelets, don't you think?"

"Oohhh, that would be good, huh?"

"Yeah."

"Let's go check?"

"Sure. You good now? Don't worry. I'll protect you from stupid fucks like that guy from before."

"Thank you," I say, kissing his cheek.

"Nah, you don't have to thank me," he says, grinning. I've never seen him grin this much, nor smile as much as he has the past few days. I like it, and I wonder if maybe he's changed after his first year of college? Maybe I've changed, too.

"You would have taken that guy down if I didn't show up. You're tough, Princess. Would have kneed the fuck right in the balls and tossed him on the ground."

"Yeah right!" I say, laughing.

I'd like to think I'm that strong. I'd like to think that Ethan actually thinks I'm that strong, too.

# 9 - Ethan

BREAKFAST IS FUCKING AMAZING. Holy fuck. Ashley is a food god. Goddess? Who the fuck knows. She's amazing, that's all. Kind of fucking obvious if you ask me, but who knows?

She's smart. Responsive as fuck. Curious and interested in sex? Yes! Fuck yes. And she's cute. Intelligent, which is different from being smart. Could work on some of her street smarts, but whatever. That's what I'm here for, right? I'll handle that shit for her, and deal with stupid punks like Johnny, too.

She's fun to hang out with, too. And really fucking cuddly. I don't like that, alright? I'm not a cuddler. I'll hold a girl a little after sex so she doesn't think I'm a completely emotionless bastard, but that's about it. Enough to get the job done, then I move on.

I want to fucking cuddle the fuck out of this girl even though we're not going to have sex. No sex? None! All fucking day. And...

Holy shit, there's something seriously wrong with me.

Yeah, well, who cares? It's just a week. I'll fix myself after that. Get back into my zone. It'll work. Don't worry about it. You worry about you, I'll worry about me. Good, glad we got that straight.

"It's really nice out today, huh?" she says after we finish eating and we're cleaning up our mess. Yeah, there's a dishwasher, but it's kind of fun cleaning and drying the dishes ourselves. Makes you feel accomplished, you know?

"Yeah. Great day." It is. Sunny as fuck.

"Do you want to go swimming?" she asks.

"I didn't think you liked swimming?" I say.

"I do, but I feel weird sometimes."

"What the fuck, why?"

"It's stupid," she says.

"It's not stupid," I say. "You can tell me."

"I'm kind of um... I know I'm not fat, but..."

"Look, Princess, you're not even close to fat."

"I'm not very athletic, though! Also I think my breasts are kind of small, don't you?"

"Are you on drugs?" Is she being serious? Yeah, they aren't huge or anything, but who the fuck wants huge breasts? I want enough to squeeze in my hands and have some fun with, but anything more isn't necessary. Ashley's got plenty.

I don't think she believes me, though. She rolls her eyes and slaps my shoulder. "You're just saying that because you want to seduce me."

"You're damn right I want to seduce you, but, nah, Princess, you're hot. You've got curves in all the right places, and, yeah, maybe you don't have girl abs or anything, but I love your stomach. And you're shaved pussy. You've got a great ass, too. And you know what? Your breasts are amazing. Maybe they aren't grossly overlarge or some shit, but I could still titfuck you pretty damn easily."

"Is this how you sweet talk all the girls?" she asks me, giggling. "You're going to have to be a little more romantic for that to work on me."

"You want romantic?" I ask, grabbing her sides. I squeeze her tight, tickling her. "I'll give you romantic, Princess. Your breasts are so nice I want to lay you down in my bed, romantically, and then straddle your stomach and thrust my cock in between your beautiful mountains and valleys while I pinch your peaked nipples of perfection."

She laughs and giggles and squirms as I tickle and tease her. This is fun. Playful as fuck, and she's cute when she smiles. Gorgeous, really. I could get used to this.

Don't get the wrong idea. I'm just saying I could.

I ease up and let her catch her breath when she starts gasping for air after laughing too hard.

"Just because--" she says, but she stops to take another breath. "Just because you say something is romantic doesn't make it romantic, Ethan. Also, your poetic purple prose is stupid. You're not going to win any poetry contests with that. I'm giving you negative points for it, too."

"Shit," I say, pretending to be seriously disappointed. Does my smile give me away? Yeah, probably. "Negative points sucks."

"It's alright," she says. "You had a lot of bonus points from yesterday, so you're still in the lead."

"Wait, who else is in this game? How much of a lead do I have?"

"Well, no one else yet, but you never know, right?"

"Shit. I need more points. How do I get more points, Princess?"

"Do you really want to know?"

"Yeah. Tell me. I'll do it, whatever it is."

She tells me. Yeah, she fucking tells me. Holy shit, Ashley is a freak. This is going to be fun.

# A NOTE FROM MIA

THIRD BOOK FINISHED. YES!

I like this one a lot. It gives a fun glimpse at Ethan and his bad boy tendencies, but maybe he's kind of nice sometimes, too. I don't know for sure. You really can't trust those bad boys, now can you?

Ashley is fun, too. I think she's cute in how naive she is sometimes. I think we can all probably remember when we were like that, too. It's fun to remember stuff like that, where we were excited and interested in things that might seem a little normal nowadays.

Maybe not too normal, haha. I can't say that I often have sex in the backseat of a car at a drive-in movie theatre. That's a little unfortunate. It sounds like a fun time. Um...

Back to book talking!

This is the middle of the book series, and I think middles are difficult sometimes, but I like this one. There was a little tension at the end with Ethan's friend, too. This secret of theirs is becoming a little complicated, don't you think? Johnny was a jerk, too, though. I'm glad that Ethan stood up for Ashley like that, but it makes you wonder if he's doing it because she's his sister or because of...?

Huh!

It's a secret. I can't tell you or it would ruin everything, now wouldn't it? You'll find out soon enough!

Thanks for reading and I hope you like how the series is going so far. It's a fun one, and it was a lot of fun to write about, too. Ashley and Ethan are getting a little weird and kinky at parts, but I kind of like it. It's alright to be freaky sometimes.

If you liked the book, I hope you'll rate and review it, too! What did you think about Ethan sticking up for Ashley against Johnny? Is he changing, or has he already changed, or is it a "once a bad boy, always a bad boy" kind of situation? I'd love to hear your thoughts!

I hope you're liking this series so far, though. There's more to come, don't worry!

Thanks for reading, and I'll see you soon! (next book!)

~MIA

# ABOUT THE AUTHOR

Mia likes to have fun in all aspects of her life. Whether she's out enjoying the beautiful weather or spending time at home reading a book, a smile is never far from her face. She's prone to randomly laughing at nothing in particular except for whatever idea amuses her at any given moment.

Sometimes you just need to enjoy life, right?

She loves to read, dance, and explore outdoors. Chamomile tea and bubble baths are two of her favorite things. Flowers are especially nice, and she could get lost in a garden if it's big enough and no one's around to remind her that there are other things to do.

She lives in New Hampshire, where the weather is beautiful and the autumn colors are amazing.

Made in the USA
San Bernardino,
CA